THE LITTLEST FROG

by Sylvia Rouss
Illustrated by Holly Hannon

PITSPOPANY

NEW YORK ◇ JERUSALEM

ANIMAL STORIES FOR CHILDREN
FROM PITSPOPANY PRESS

Seven Animal Stories For Children
by Howard and Mary K. Bogot

Seven Animals Wag Their Tales
by Howard and Mary K. Bogot

The Rooster Prince
Retold by Sydell Waxman

Published by Pitspopany Press
Text copyright © 2001 by Sylvia Rouss
Illustrations copyright © 2001 by Holly Hannon

Design: Benjie Herskowitz

ISBN: 1-930143-12-5

Pitspopany Press titles may be purchased for fund raising programs
by schools and organizations by contacting:
Marketing Director, Pitspopany Press
40 East 78" Street, Suite 16D, New York, New York 10021
Tel: (800) 232 2931
Fax: (212) 472 6253
Email: pop@netvision.net.il
Web Site: www.pitspopany.com

Printed in Israel

To my husband, Jeff,
for his encouragement and support

S.R.

Unusual Words

Pharaoh – title of the ancient Egyptian Kings

Scepter – a long pole decorated with jewels held
   by a King

Papyrus – a plant that was used to make paper
   in ancient Egypt

Urn – a clay pot

Hieroglyphics – ancient Egyptian writing using
   pictures instead of letters

In Egypt, long ago...

Moses and Aaron went to Pharaoh.

"Let my people go," Moses said, "or God will make millions of frogs come out of the Nile River and jump all over your land."

But Pharaoh wouldn't listen.

So Aaron stretched his staff over the water, and millions, even billions, maybe zillions of frogs jumped out of the Nile River and into the houses, beds, sheds, pots, bowls, and even the ovens of the Egyptians.

Pharaoh's magicians could also make frogs appear, but they couldn't make them disappear.

There were frogs everywhere!

From THE JEWISH CHILDREN'S BIBLE
Adapted by Sheryl Prenzlau (Pitspopany Press)

A little frog sat in the hot Egyptian sun,
Watching Jewish slaves work, while Pharaoh had fun.

Moses, their leader, warned evil Pharaoh,
"Bad things will happen if you don't let us go."

"I'm the great Pharaoh and nothing scares me!
The Jewish people will stay! They'll never be free!"

The very next morning, when Pharaoh arose,
He found a big frog, sitting right on his nose.

"Pyramids!" he yelled, as he jumped up in fright.
There were frogs to his left and frogs to his right.

He grabbed for his sandals and to his surprise,
Sitting there was a frog with big bulgy eyes.

"Oh no!" he exclaimed as he pulled on his gown.
There was a bullfrog wearing his crown!

There were frogs in all sizes, hopping about.
The biggest ones made Pharaoh tremble and shout.

But the littlest frog was very afraid.
He hid under the bed, and that's where he stayed.

Pharaoh ran to his bath, and grabbed a large towel.
But when he got there, he let out a howl.

There in his bath, frogs were taking a swim,
Doing the backstroke, and staring at him.

He fled to the kitchen and opened the door.
There were frogs on the table, frogs on the floor.

Oh such a sight, Pharaoh never had seen.
Wherever he looked, he saw only green.

He sped through the palace and let out a groan.
There were frogs on his scepter and frogs on his throne.

There were frogs on the curtains and in the fruit bowls.
There were frogs peeking out from papyrus scrolls.

He saw frogs on the ceiling and frogs on the wall.
He saw frogs in each room and down every hall.

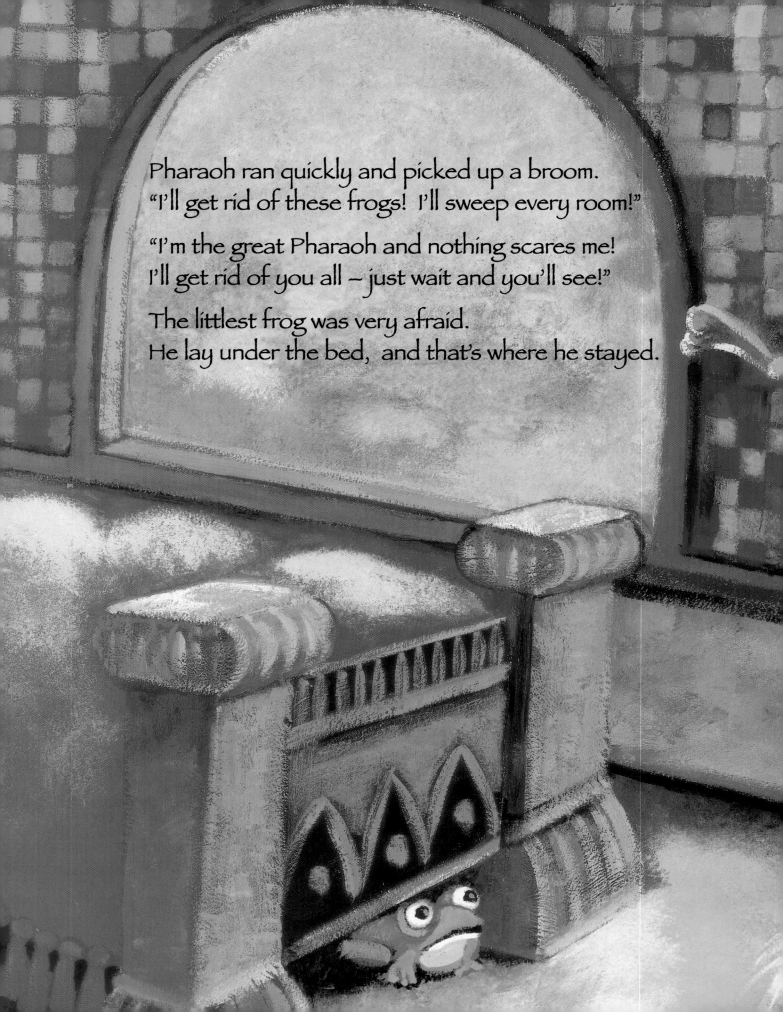

Pharaoh ran quickly and picked up a broom.
"I'll get rid of these frogs! I'll sweep every room!"

"I'm the great Pharaoh and nothing scares me!
I'll get rid of you all – just wait and you'll see!"

The littlest frog was very afraid.
He lay under the bed, and that's where he stayed.

Pharaoh checked every basket and shook out each rug.
He looked in the urns and emptied each jug.

Wherever he looked, frogs were hopping and leaping.
Pharaoh snarled at them all and continued his sweeping.

As he swept one last frog from the top of a shelf,
Pharaoh felt happy and pleased with himself.

"I got rid of you all!" he gleefully cried.
"There's nowhere left for you frogs to hide!"

The littlest frog was very afraid.
He lay under the bed, and that's where he stayed.

Pharaoh shut every door, and felt very proud.
In hieroglyphics he wrote,
"NO FROGS ALLOWED!"

"I'm tired," he sighed, and with one final sweep,
He crawled into bed and fell fast asleep.

When the palace was quiet and peaceful at last,
When the shutters were drawn and the doors all shut fast,

The littlest frog was no longer afraid.
He hopped onto Pharaoh, and that's where he stayed.

Now it was safe, so he bellowed a "CROAK!"
And just at that moment, the Pharaoh awoke.

"This can't be happening! This must be a dream!
I got rid of you frogs!" Pharaoh began to scream.

He arose from his bed with a terrible thought –
"Can this be what my stubbornness has brought?!"

"Perhaps Moses was right, the Jews should be free.
Maybe that's why this is happening to me."

Suddenly, Pharaoh was very afraid.
He hid under the bed, and that's where he stayed!